Nooruk Safar

Mutahir Showkat

In the darkest hours, even a flicker of light can guide the lost. This is Nooruk Safar a journey toward the dawn of the soul.

Copyright

Introduction

Nooruk Safar is a heartfelt story about facing life's toughest times and finding hope, even in darkness. Based on true events, it explores how people can lose their way, fall into troubling situations, and feel overwhelmed by emotions they never expected. This story is about the journey through difficult moments moments of fear, regret, and choices that sometimes bring pain.

The characters, places, and events in this book are all imagined by the author to connect with readers who may have faced similar struggles. While some parts might feel familiar, any likeness to actual people or real events is purely accidental.

This story is not about promoting anyone or any place; it's simply about showing the strength, courage, and hope that can be found in even the darkest of times. Through the characters' ups and downs, Nooruk Safar reminds us that no matter how lost we feel, there's always a path toward light, healing, and self discovery.

Summary

Nooruk Safar tells the story of an innocent boy from Kashmir who makes new friends, leading him to experience the challenges of life. As he gets caught up in a haram relationship, he loses his peace and innocence. This toxic relationship pushes him toward drugs, leading him into addiction.

Eventually, he realises how far he has fallen from being a respected member of his family to losing his reputation and self-worth. In a moment of despair, he kneels before his Lord, seeking help and a fresh start.

This marks the beginning of a new life for him. As he tries to rebuild, he meets someone who plays an important role in his transformation. Through this journey, he discovers love again, and this experience shapes his path moving forward.

About the Author

Mutahir Showkat is an Indian entrepreneur, author, and crypto enthusiast who crafts stories reflecting the emotions and experiences of everyday life. His writing resonates with readers, capturing the complexities of human feelings and relationships.

In his previous work, Shadows That Shape Us Too, Mutahir explored themes of resilience and personal growth, illustrating how individuals navigate life's challenges. Through his storytelling, he aims to inspire and connect with people from diverse backgrounds, offering valuable insights in a rapidly evolving world.

www.mutahir.xyz

contact@mutahir.xyz

Note from the Author

This book may not meet everyone's expectations. I know I'm
not a well-known author, and sometimes I may not use the
perfect words. I'm just an ordinary writer who often makes
mistakes, but I've tried my best to create something
meaningful for you.

For the first time, I want to share that before writing this
book, I was somewhat distant in my faith, questioning
things around me. As I started writing these chapters, I
found myself turning to verses from the Quran. I can't quite
explain it, but something changed in my life. I began to feel a
sense of peace, and I started connecting with Allah in ways I
hadn't before. Writing this book may be a small
achievement, but it has truly transformed me.

This story might seem simple or not very exciting to some,
but for me, it has been life changing. Alhamdulillah.

"And whoever fears Allah - He will make for him a way out
and will provide for him from where he does not expect."
— Quran, Surah At-Talaq (65:2-3)

.

A Note on Language and Meaning

In this book, you'll find the use of multiple languages Arabic, Kashmiri, Urdu, and English blending together to bring authenticity and depth to the story. While the words are presented in English spellings for easier reading, the meanings of Arabic, Urdu and Kashmiri words are provided in brackets for clarity.

The author acknowledges that, as the languages may not be perfectly transcribed into English, there might be variations in tone or spelling. Any such errors are unintentional, and the author deeply apologizes for them. The intention is to connect readers with the essence of the story while respecting the beauty of each language.

Seoud Te Saadeh

"Keep your heart pure, for every soul is born with innocence, and indeed, it is Allah who guides to the straight path."

From the moment he woke up, he embraced each day with a heart full of purity. Life was simple, but in that simplicity lay his joy. He had a way of making each morning feel like a blessing, and he greeted every new day with gratitude. His home was a warm and loving place where respect and care were woven into daily life, and he was at the heart of it all.

Each day began with the soothing ritual of wudhu. He would gently splash cool water over his face, feeling refreshed and prepared for his first prayer. Then he would go to the masjid near his home with his Baba (father). Standing next to his Baba, he would wait as Imaam Soab (the Imam of the masjid) began the salah. While offering namaz beside his Baba Jaan, facing the qibla, he felt a calmness settle over him. The quiet of the early morning filled him with peace as he whispered verses from the Quran, feeling a connection that steadied his heart. 'Indeed, in the remembrance of Allah do hearts find rest' (Quran 13:28).

After his morning prayers, he would go to the kitchen, where his Mouj would be waiting for his Baba Jaan and him. When they entered the kitchen, she would often say, 'Aakeih aaw meon khanmoal' (here comes my proud son). Then, she would offer them cups of noon chai (Kashmiri tea) and a Lawas (Kashmiri bread). After the chai, he would step outside, embracing the crisp air as it brushed against his face. The early sunlight crept over the mountains, casting a golden glow across the valley, illuminating the Chinar trees, their leaves gently swaying. He would pause, taking in the sight of the morning sun touching everything it could reach, and say, 'Khodai senz niyamat' (Allah's blessing) as a prayer of thanks for the beauty around him.

Seoud Te Saadeh

In his family, he was known for his gentle nature and kindness. His parents often looked at him with pride, watching him grow into a young man with a respectful heart and a genuine love for others. His mother, with her soft eyes and warm smile, would often tell him, "Myani Gobra! Dil gasi saaf thavun, ye che baed niyamat" (A pure heart is the greatest treasure, my son. Keep it safe.)

He took these words to heart, finding ways each day to make a small difference in the lives of others. He loved helping those around him, and his village was like an extended family. At the market, he would carry groceries for elderly neighbours, listening patiently as they spoke of their own youth, their memories mingling with his present. These simple acts brought him happiness, filling him with a sense of purpose.

Whenever he met elders, he greeted them with respect, bowing his head in a slight nod and offering a kind word. The older men would pat his back, their voices warm as they blessed him. "Khodai thavnei hamesha reche wateh peth" (May you continue on this right path,") they would say. He would smile in return, feeling honoured to earn their blessings.

"A heart so soft, like morning dew,
Reflecting skies of purest blue.
In deeds so small, kindness grows,
As life's true path through love shows."

Seoud Te Saadeh

He loved to sit by Dal Lake in the evenings, watching the boats as they drifted gently across the water. The lake was calm, its surface reflecting the vibrant colours of the setting sun. There was a quiet magic here, a beauty that made him feel connected to something larger than himself. He would close his eyes, breathe in the fresh air, and let his mind settle. For him, these moments of stillness were like silent prayers, a way of appreciating the world Allah had created.

"In every breath, a gift so rare,
Allah's mercy fills the air.
From sky to earth, His blessings flow,
Reminding us in whispers slow."

His days were full, yet peaceful. Each task was done with care, each interaction marked by thoughtfulness. He found joy in little things: feeding the birds that gathered in his yard, watching children play in the fields, and listening to the call of the azan as it echoed across the valley. Every sound, every scent, every sight felt like a reminder of Allah's mercy, and he held these reminders close to his heart.

In his own family, he was the gentle soul who listened more than he spoke, offering quiet comfort when others needed it. If his siblings faced difficulties, he was there with a kind word and an open ear. He knew that family was a bond created by Allah, something to be treasured and protected. His mother would often tell him, "Khandaan chu rehmat, teh amech izzat rachen ti che ibaadat "Family is a blessing, and respect for it is an act of worship."

Seoud Te Saadeh

On weekends, he would accompany his family to visit relatives. These gatherings were filled with laughter and joy, the air thick with the scent of Nun chai (Kashmiri tea) and girdeh (Kashmiri bread). He enjoyed these moments, surrounded by cousins and uncles, each sharing stories and laughter. The elders would often talk about the "Kujaa Soan Waqt," (their old days) and he would sit quietly, absorbing every tale as if it were a lesson in living a good life.

After the meal, he would sometimes walk to the garden with his grandfather, a wise man with a soft voice and gentle hands that seemed to carry years of patience. His grandfather would talk of the land, the trees, and the simple beauty of hard work. He would say, "Zindagi Che yeman kulen hend paeth, yem dabeth che imanas manz teh asmans watnukh chukh shoakh, panin mooel gasen thaven daeid teh che mili kamyabi" (Life is like these trees, rooted in faith and reaching for the sky. Keep your roots strong, and you will grow in the right way.)

"In fields of green and skies so wide,
The seeds of love in hearts reside.
From earth to sky, our prayers rise,
A grateful heart, the best prize."

One winter morning, after the first snowfall, he decided to walk down to the village square. Everything was covered in a blanket of white, and the valley was silent, as if holding its breath. The cold air was sharp, filling his lungs with a freshness that made him feel alive. He saw children laughing, throwing snowballs at each other, their cheeks red with cold. He smiled at their joy, feeling a sense of warmth despite the chill.

Seoud Te Saadeh

During these quiet days, he often visited the masjid. The masjid was a sanctuary for him, a place where he felt truly at peace. He would sit there in silence, his heart light as he spoke to Allah in soft whispers. The masjid walls held the prayers of generations, and he felt honoured to be part of that line of faith. "And whoever relies upon Allah, He is sufficient for him" (Quran 65:3). These words echoed in his heart, filling him with strength.

As the seasons changed, he found beauty in each one. Spring brought vibrant colours to the valley, with flowers blooming along the paths he walked. Summer was warm and gentle, with long days spent outdoors, helping his father in the fields or visiting relatives. Autumn brought the golden hues of the Chinar trees, and he would watch as their leaves floated to the ground, like little pieces of sunlight falling to earth. Winter, with its quiet beauty, was a time for reflection, for sitting close to the fire and listening to his family's stories.

> "Seasons pass, yet hearts remain,
> Through joy and sorrow, love sustains.
> Like leaves that fall, we rise anew,
> Guided by the faith we pursue."

In his heart, he carried a simple joy and gratitude for the life he had. He knew that each day, each season, was a gift. This understanding shaped his actions, filling him with a quiet strength that shone through his words and deeds.

Whenever he passed by neighbours, they would greet him warmly. He was known as a boy of good character, someone who lived with kindness and humility. His presence was like a gentle light, and people often looked to him as an example of how one should live. The village women would say, 'Saanen shuren karetan ame sund heow hidayat' (our children should be blessed like him.)

"A heart that's pure, like morning's dew,
Reflects a love that's strong and true.
In simple acts, his light is shown,
A path of peace, a life well-known."

For him, happiness was in the small things, the laughter of family, the peace of prayer, the beauty of the valley, and the warmth of human connection. His days were not just about routine they were about cherishing what he had, finding meaning in the everyday, and recognising the blessings that surrounded him.

And as he went to sleep each night, he would offer a final prayer, asking Allah to keep his heart pure, to help him stay on the path of goodness. He was grateful, humble, and hopeful, trusting that as long as he remained close to his faith, he would continue to live a life of peace

"In Allah's light, I find my way,
Through every night, to each new day.
A grateful heart, a gentle hand,
Forever guided by His command."

Seoud Te Saadeh

In the garden of youth, where dreams take flight,
A heart so pure, bathed in morning light.
With every laugh, a sweet melody,
In the warmth of love, two souls feel free.

"Allah, show us the way," they gently pray,
Guided by faith in the brightening day.
In the green valleys, where Chinar trees sway,
Their hearts dance together, come what may.

A story of love, a tale of grace,
In the soft whispers, they find their place.
Kashmiri skies, painted with bright hues,
Hold the secrets of love in the night's views.

As they dream of tomorrow, with hope in their hearts,
They trust in the journey where each story starts.
With prayers on their lips, they cherish the bliss,
In the world of love, they find their peace.

"You are the light," they often say,
In the joy of togetherness, come what may.
With Allah's blessings, they sing their own song,
In the fabric of life, they know they belong.

Seoud Te Saadeh

NOVV HAWA

"A new air breathes life into forgotten dreams, lifting the soul toward paths unknown."

Novv Hawah

One late evening, as he sat by Dal Lake, enjoying the peace of the night, he didn't know his world was about to change. The lake was quiet, the gentle lapping of water against the shikara boats the only sound breaking the silence. The sky was draped in soft starlight, with the Chinar trees silhouetted against it, their leaves barely rustling in the calm night. This place had always been his refuge, a sacred space where he could reflect and let his heart rest in gratitude.

> "In the stillness of night, whispers sway,
> Bringing change, in soft, unseen ways.
> Like winds that shift, beyond control,
> Stirring heart, mind, and soul."

As he looked at the next ghat of Dal Lake, he noticed a group of young men and women laughing nearby. Their voices, full of energy and life, were unlike the familiar quiet of his own friends and family. Drawn by their laughter, he watched them from a distance, observing their carefree movements, the way they seemed completely absorbed in their own world. One of them noticed him, and with a friendly wave, called him over. 'Kyahaw baya, wala beh aaseh nish' (What's good, bro? Come here and sit with us.)

Curiosity awakened within him. His steps were hesitant at first, but something in their ease and laughter felt welcoming, as if they held a secret he didn't yet know. When he approached, they greeted him warmly, as if he were an old friend rather than a stranger. Their smiles were genuine, open, and he felt a small thrill at the thought of this unexpected companionship.

Novv Hawah

One of the young men reached into his pocket and pulled out a small box, offering him a cigarette with a smile. 'Baya, cigarette chekha?' (Bro, would you like to smoke a cigarette?). He hesitated, feeling the weight of his upbringing and values in that single moment. The scent of the cigarette was foreign to him, unfamiliar and slightly unsettling. With a polite smile, he shook his head, declining the offer. 'Buh chus neh chewan' (I don't smoke), he replied. They shrugged, not offended by his choice, and simply laughed it off.

One of the girls in the group teased, "Enhhh acha che chukh asul shur" (So, you're the good boy, huh?)" She said it with a laugh, but there was something in her voice, something that hinted he was missing out on something. The words struck him unexpectedly, leaving a faint question lingering in his mind. Was he a good boy? What did that mean? And did it mean he was missing out on something else?

They moved on to other topics, chatting about places they'd been, people they knew, and the latest trends in fashion and music. 'Aap nai MC Kash ka naya gaana suna?' (Did you hear the new song by MC Kash?) one of the girls asked. He stayed silent. Meanwhile, another person next to him said, 'Alai, MC Kash chu kalleh rapper' (Hey, MC Kash is the great rapper). Their world seemed so different from his own, full of excitement and energy, a stark contrast to the steady life he led. The way they spoke so freely, laughing without restraint, held a strange attraction. He listened, feeling both drawn in and cautious, trying to balance his curiosity with the values he had always held close.

"When winds of change start to blow,
Unknown paths begin to show.
The heart feels a stirring deep,
Awakened dreams from restful sleep."

They asked him about his life, his friends, his family, and even about relationships. One of the boys laughed and said, 'Kyasa chobra cha kanh?' (So, do you have a girlfriend?). This question embarrassed him, it was likely the first time someone had asked him something like this, and he just felt lost. The same person continued, 'Kyahav bhai, dopmai relationship chaya?' (Bro, I asked if you're in a relationship). The question caught him off guard. For him, relationships were a matter of families, and he wasn't much into those things. He stayed calm and replied, 'Naa baya' (no, brother). But deep inside, he was constantly thinking about it how could a person he had just met ask him questions like these? Was this just a normal part of their routine? He even found himself wondering if he was missing something from his life. Was his life old fashioned?

He found himself wondering if he was missing something in life, feeling a bit lost. Deep inside, he was asking himself, 'Myani Khodaya, ye cha aam kath?' (Oh my Lord, is this just normal talk?). He had never thought about relationships in this way never really considered love or romance as something that could just happen or be casually discussed. His understanding of relationships was shaped by what he had seen around him his parents' bond, rooted in respect and care. This idea of casually asking about relationships felt entirely new to him.

Novv Hawah

One of the boys chuckled, slapping him lightly on the shoulder. 'Wala baya, che te haa aasi jaldi chober' (Don't worry, man, you'll also have a girlfriend soon). The group laughed, and he felt a mixture of amusement and curiosity, feeling like a part of their world while still being slightly apart from it. They seemed so certain, so at ease with these ideas. Their words lingered in his mind, planting a small seed of wonder.

As the evening wore on, he listened more than he spoke, absorbing their stories, their laughter, the way they seemed to drift from one moment to the next. He realised they saw life differently, that they approached each day with a kind of freedom he hadn't known. For them, life wasn't something to be carefully planned, but something to experience fully, without restraint.

> "A gentle breeze, a whispered dare,
> To leave the known, the comfort shared.
> For in new paths, the soul may grow,
> Learning truths it didn't know."

When it was time to leave, they waved him off with the same warmth they had greeted him with, calling out for him to meet them again sometime. He walked away, feeling a sense of excitement mixed with uncertainty. He had always known himself as the 'boy with values,' the one who followed the rules and stayed close to his family's values. Yet here, in one evening, he had glimpsed a life that held an unfamiliar pull, a life that seemed both thrilling and bewildering.

Novv Hawah

Over the next few days, his thoughts often drifted back to that evening. He replayed their laughter, their words, and the casual way they spoke about relationships and fun. He found himself wondering what it would be like to experience that kind of freedom, to laugh without worry, to see life as a series of moments rather than a series of duties.

> "Innocence sways, to a tune unknown,
> A whispered path, by winds shown.
> Curiosity blooms, like a flower's call,
> In the shadows where questions fall."

He returned to Dal Lake, hoping to find them there again. It wasn't just the attraction of their company, but the pull of something new, something that promised a different perspective on life. When he found them, they greeted him with the same easy warmth, pulling him into their circle as if he had always belonged.

They laughed and joked, sharing stories and ideas that left him both amused and thoughtful. He realised there were parts of life he had never considered, that there was a whole world beyond the peaceful routines he had known. With every conversation, every laugh, he felt a part of himself awakening, as if something within him was stirring, eager to explore these new thoughts.

As days passed, he spent more time with them. He still held on to his values, resisting anything that felt too far from the person he was, but he enjoyed their company, their energy. They showed him a world where enjoyment didn't have to be measured, where moments were embraced fully. And in their laughter, he felt a freedom he had not known before, a sense that life could hold surprises and unknown paths.

> "To see the world with new eyes clear,
> Where innocence meets edges near.
> A path unknown, where whispers lie,
> Beneath the stars in open sky."

Yet, as he stood on the edge of this new world, he found himself constantly looking back, feeling the gentle pull of home, the familiar comfort of his prayers, his family, and the quiet moments of reflection. He knew he was at a threshold, that he could either step forward into a new chapter or turn back to the life he had always known.

But the winds of influence had begun to touch him, and he could feel their gentle nudge each time he returned to the lake, each time he heard their laughter. A small part of him wanted to know more, to understand the world they saw, to experience a life where questions could be asked and boundaries explored.

As he walked back home that night, his mind swirled with questions, the kind that don't find answers in silence. He realised that change was like the wind gentle at first, almost unnoticed, but capable of carrying seeds that could grow into something unexpected. And though he was still the boy with a kind heart and gentle soul, he sensed that a new journey had begun, one he couldn't quite turn away from.

"In winds that bring new thoughts to bear,
The heart learns paths both rich and rare.
A seed of wonder, quietly sown,
As the boy steps into the unknown."

Novv Hawah

In the soft evening light, where shadows play,
New faces appear, turning night into day.
By the shores of Dal, where laughter flows,
He meets fresh breezes, and his heart starts to glow.

"Come join our circle," they say with delight,
In the moon's warm glow, everything feels right.
With drinks in hand, excitement takes flight,
But a little voice warns him in the night.

In the dance of young friends, he feels a spark,
A friendship begins in the calm, still dark.
The joy of youth shines bright in their cheer,
In their stories and laughter, he finds what is dear.

"How lovely life is!" they sing with glee,
In the winds of change, he feels happy and free.
Curiosity blooms, like flowers in spring,
With every new moment, his heart starts to sing.

As the night deepens and shadows blend,
He finds a path where his heart can mend.
With a heart full of questions, he takes a leap,
In the world of new faces, his soul starts to creep.

Novv Hawah

Sangatuk Asar

"Like the unseen hand of the wind,
some moments pass through our lives,
shifting our hearts and changing our
paths in ways we never expected."

As the days passed, he found himself drawn deeper into the world of his new friends, the group that had opened his eyes to a life he had barely known existed. Every gathering with them brought fresh laughter, new adventures, and a sense of belonging that had become strangely essential to him. They met regularly, often by the banks of Dal Lake, under the stars that watched over their laughter and shared moments.

In one of those gatherings, he met her.

It was an ordinary evening, with conversations flowing easily among the group, a chorus of voices blending with the quiet murmur of the lake. She had been a part of the group for a while, but they had only exchanged polite smiles and casual greetings. That night, however, she seemed closer, sitting just across from him, her laughter carrying a lightness that made his heart feel an unfamiliar pull. Her presence was like a subtle breeze that shifts unexpectedly, catching you off guard.

One of the girls in the group noticed his gaze staying on her and leaned in with a mischievous smile. she teased, nudging him gently. "Che maa aayi ye pasand" (Oh, I guess you liked her?).

He felt warmth creep into his cheeks, a shy smile playing on his lips as he turned away, but not before stealing another glance at her. Her face held a quiet beauty, her eyes reflecting the warmth of the night around them. He didn't say anything, but his heart spoke a language he hadn't known it could. It was as if something deep inside him had been awakened, a feeling so new yet so fascinating that he found himself pulled into it without fighting back.

Sangatuk Asar

"A heart untouched, now finds its beat,
In a glance so pure, and love so sweet.
Like rain on earth, it blooms anew,
A love unknown, yet deeply true."

That night, as he lay in bed, his mind kept drifting back to her. Her laughter echoed in his memory, her smile became a gentle ache in his heart. The feeling was almost overwhelming, something he couldn't explain to himself. He found his thoughts wrapped around her presence, the way she had looked at him, the sound of her laughter mixing with the whispers of the lake. It was as if he had found a part of himself he hadn't known was missing.

Soon, she became a part of his conversations with the group, especially in their late-night WhatsApp chats. His friends teased him, playfully nudging him to share more about his feelings for her. They would send him cheeky emojis, asking him if he had spoken to her, if he had found an excuse to sit by her side, or if he had managed to catch her attention with his shy smiles. He would laugh, brushing it off, but a quiet excitement stayed in his heart, a thrill that only he knew.

One evening, one of the girls from the group, who was close to her, mentioned that she had spoken to her about him. His heart skipped a beat. She had talked to her about him? The thought filled him with a nervous excitement, a hope that maybe she had noticed him in the same way he had noticed her. He didn't ask for more details, but every word of encouragement from his friend felt like a piece of sunlight slipping into his life, warming him from within.

Sangatuk Asar

"Love's first touch, so soft and shy,
Like morning mist beneath the sky.
In whispered words and stolen glances,
A heart awakened, as love advances."

He began seeing her in everything in the quiet beauty of dawn, in the gentle ripples on the lake, in the delicate petals of flowers that lined his path. Every day felt brighter, every moment fuller, as if his world had taken on a richer hue. This was a feeling he hadn't known before, something entirely his own. He felt like the innocent boy he had always been, yet somehow different, somehow awakened.

In their next meeting at Nishat Bagh, he found himself drawn to her side. She looked at him, her gaze calm yet curious, and for a moment, the world around them faded into silence. They talked about simple things about the stars above them, the beauty of the Nishat Bagh, the familiar places they both knew in Kashmir. Her words were like a gentle song, her voice soft and comforting, each syllable carving a place in his heart.

With each meeting, his feelings grew stronger. He found himself thinking about her throughout the day, his mind wandering to the smallest details about her the way she tucked her hair behind her ear when she laughed, the warmth in her eyes when she spoke. The world seemed to shrink to just her, and everything else felt secondary, distant.

"In silence, hearts begin to know,
A feeling pure, with gentle glow.
Like rivers meet and blend unseen,
A love that grows, quiet yet keen."

His friends noticed the change in him, playfully calling him out for being lost in his thoughts and for smiling at nothing in particular. "Bayi's chu love gomut" (Brother is in love), they would often say. He would laugh, pretending to brush off their teasing, but deep down, he knew there was truth in their words. This feeling had taken root in him, spreading through his soul like the warmth of spring after a long winter.

One evening, as they sat together in their usual spot, his friend shared with him a message from her. She had spoken to her, shared with her about his feelings, and in return, she had smiled, saying, "Walah wuchawai khodyan kya aaseh likhith thomut" (Let's see what Allah has planned). The words were simple, but to him, they held an entire world of possibility. While he was lost in thought, a guy next to him said, "Alai bayis gov love kamyaab" (Oh brother, love is successful).

From that moment, he felt a quiet determination. He wanted to be the best version of himself, not just for her, but for this feeling that had blossomed within him. He wanted to be worthy of her gaze, to be the kind of person she could trust, respect, and maybe one day, even care for. His prayers became more sincere, his kindness more intentional, and his actions more thoughtful.

Sangatuk Asar

"In love's light, the heart refines,
Becoming pure, as gold in fire shines.
A love that asks, yet does not take,
A love so deep, for its own sake."

Days passed, and he would see her in their gatherings, each time stealing glances, each time hoping she might look his way. Every interaction felt sacred, every word a treasure he held close. He knew he was still the innocent boy from before, but he had found a new purpose, a new joy in simply thinking of her.

He didn't rush, didn't try to confess his feelings right away. Instead, he let the love grow, quietly, like a rose that blooms in its own time. He held onto every moment with her, every shared smile, every conversation, as if they were gifts meant only for him.

"In patience, love finds strength to wait,
To grow in time, to bloom in fate.
For love that's true, endures the test,
And holds each moment as its best."

His friends continued to tease him, saying, "Boi chu baneowmut, majnu" (brother has become Majnu), yet they also encouraged him, reminding him that love, like life, was meant to be cherished. "Bhai akh kath wanhoi love bagair chane zindagi kehin te" (bro, we would say one thing: without love, life is nothing). He knew he was on a path that was both thrilling and unknown, and though he couldn't see where it would lead, he was content to simply let his heart guide him, one step at a time.

Sangatuk Asar

In her presence, he felt as if he had found a part of himself that had always been waiting. She became a reason for him to dream, a quiet joy that coloured his days and lifted his spirit. And as he walked along the banks of Dal Lake, the same place where he had first met her, he realised that he had fallen, deeply and quietly, into a love he couldn't deny.

Sangatuk Asar

In the air, a soft whisper, a sweet serenade,
Among friends and laughter, new feelings cascade.
A quick glance catches his eye, like a gentle spark,
In his heart's hidden space, love lights up the dark.

The Chinar leaves sway in a beautiful dance,
With each beat of his heart, he's lost in a trance.
In a joyful circle where friendships are tight,
He dreams of her laughter as the stars shine bright.

In the valleys where moonlight glows,
Her presence fills his thoughts, a feeling that grows.
With feelings unspoken, his heart starts to rise,
In the garden of emotions, he longs for her sighs.

A beautiful love, shining and pure,
He finds himself trapped in feelings so sure.
Through messages they share, their hearts start to show,
In the tapestry of youth, a new story will flow.

With every heartbeat, he searches for her trace,
In the warmth of their chats, his heart finds its place.
But in the shadows, a question takes flight:
Is this love that he feels, or just a sweet delight?

As the world keeps spinning, he smiles with glee,
In this glow of affection, everything feels free.
With love's sweet obsession, he's ready to dare,
In the realm of the heart, he's caught unaware.

Sangatuk Asar

Dilaech Gaflat

"A heart entangled in forbidden love loses its peace, for true love is found only in the purity of nikah. Haraam relationships may tempt, but they only lead to a restless soul."

As the days turned into weeks, their bond deepened, weaving itself into the fabric of their lives in a way that felt both existing and daunting. What had started as innocent laughter and shared glances gradually morphed into something much more intense a connection that vibrated with excitement yet carried the weight of unspoken consequences. Their conversations, once light hearted and playful, took on a new tone, heavy with longing and whispered secrets.

He found himself captivated by her, drawn to the way she could light up his world with just a few words. Their late night calls became the highlight of his day, each conversation stretching into the early hours of the morning as they spoke about everything and nothing at all. In those moments, he felt as if they existed in their own universe, separate from the expectations and responsibilities that rose over them.

Yet, amid the thrill of their growing intimacy, a shadow remained. The teachings of Islam echoed in his mind, reminding him of the boundaries that should not be crossed. He thought of the Quranic verses that warned against temptation and sin:

"And do not follow the footsteps of Satan. And whoever follows the footsteps of Satan indeed, he enjoins what is unlawful and immoral."
(Surah Al-Baqarah, 2:168)

But the pull of their connection was powerful, blurring the lines of right and wrong. They began to spend more time alone, drifting away from their group, seeking solace in the quiet corners of beautiful places.

Dilaech Gaflat

Pahalgam, with its serene rivers and majestic mountains, became their hideaway. Gulmarg, with its enchanting meadows and snow capped peaks, served as a backdrop for stolen moments that felt too precious to be real.

In the depths of his heart, he wrestled with the dichotomy of his feelings. The joy of being with her was intoxicating, yet it was accompanied by an uneasy conscience. He often recalled the saying that sometimes, haraam things taste sweet, and in those moments, he could not deny the truth of it. The thrill of sneaking away, the excitement of secret meetings, and the warmth of her presence wrapped around him like a soft blanket, despite the chill of impending consequences.

"But they who disbelieve and commit sins are in a grave error."
(Surah Al-Anfal, 8:22)

They bunked classes. "Kya gasav college, pakh gasav Pahalgam?" (Why go to college? Let's go to Pahalgam) he would often say, sometimes slipping away to enjoy the beauty of nature, lost in the lush landscapes that mirrored the intensity of their emotions. Each adventure was a whirlwind of laughter and stolen kisses, yet beneath the surface lay an undercurrent of tension. They knew they were traversing a path deemed forbidden by their faith, yet the allure of their relationship blinded them to the warnings echoing in their hearts.

The nights grew longer as they wandered through the quiet streets of Raj Bagh, the moonlight casting soft shadows that danced around them. Their conversations often shifted to the future, with hopes and dreams mingling with a sense of uncertainty.

Dilaech Gaflat

They spoke of traveling together, of experiencing life beyond the borders of Kashmir, of building a world that revolved solely around each other. But with each word, the weight of their reality pressed heavier upon him.

Yet, the more they enjoyed their time together, the more distant he became from his friends. The laughter that once filled their gatherings began to fade into silence. He realised he was no longer present, mentally or emotionally. He found himself often distracted, his thoughts drifting to her when he should have been focused on the camaraderie he once cherished. They would plan outings that excluded the group, escaping to secluded spots where they could enjoy their forbidden bond without judgment.

His heart raced with every secret meeting, but so did the voice of doubt. It whispered of the consequences, the sins that were piling up like snow in the mountains beautiful yet dangerous. He would try to rationalise their actions, convincing himself that their love was genuine, that it transcended the rules that governed their lives. But deep inside, he knew the truth.

"Indeed, Shaitan (Satan) is an enemy to you, so take him as an enemy." (Surah Al-Fatir, 35:6)

Each moment spent away from their friends felt like a step further into a world that was both amazing and terrifying. They began to indulge in things that felt forbidden sharing secrets and feelings that shouldn't have been spoken in the first place. With each new adventure came a sense of exhilaration, but also a creeping fear of what they were becoming.

Dilaech Gaflat

Seasons changed, and with them, he could feel the innocence of their love slipping away. The joy that once illuminated his heart was gradually being replaced by a shadow of guilt. He remembered the teachings of his faith, the importance of self control and righteousness, and he wondered if he was losing a part of himself to this haraam bond.

As they roamed the hills of Daksum, he found himself at a crossroads. The thrilling moments spent together were overshadowed by the understanding that what they were doing was not just looked down upon but deeply wrong. In the quiet moments, he would catch himself thinking about the significance of the choices they were making.

"Indeed, Allah does not change the condition of a people until they change what is in themselves." (Surah Ar-Ra'd, 13:11)

Despite the thrill that came with their secret, he could no longer ignore the growing unease in his heart. The whispers of his conscience grew louder, battling against the sweetness of the moments they shared. Every sunset they witnessed together felt like a fleeting goodbye, a reminder that nothing was forever, and everything came with a price.

He knew that love should not be harmed by secrecy or sin, and as he walked the path they had chosen, he began to question everything. Was this bond worth the risk of losing his faith, his friends, and ultimately, himself? With each passing day, the sweetness of their bond felt increasingly bittersweet, a stark contrast to the laughter and joy that once defined their connection.

Dilaech Gaflat

In the depths of his soul, he realised that their love had morphed into something unrecognisable, a dangerous dance with temptation that threatened to consume him. With a heavy heart, he faced the truth that this forbidden bond might lead to a breaking point a moment where choices would have to be made, where the joy of love would either redeem him or drag him deeper into darkness.

"And those who believe are stronger in love for Allah." (Surah Al-Baqarah, 2:165)

The path ahead was unclear, and as he gazed into the distance, he knew he would have to confront the reality of their relationship. The seasons would continue to change, but he hoped to find the strength within himself to navigate the winding roads of love and faith, before it was too late.

Dilaech Gaflat

In the shadows, they stay, a bond kept away,
Hearts connected in a dance, hidden from the day.
With laughter and secrets, they drift from the crowd,
In the quiet of longing, their feelings speak loud.

"This love isn't easy," the heart whispers low,
Yet in every secret moment, their feelings start to grow.
From quiet talks to glances that spark,
In the maze of love, they've wandered far in the dark.

"Stay away," warns the voice of reason inside,
But the heart seeks the thrill, in the storms they abide.
In the glow of twilight, temptation starts to rise,
As they chase after shadows, ignoring the wise.

In the valleys where wishes take flight,
They find comfort in chaos, turning from the light.
Yet the whispers of conscience echo in their mind,
As they taste the sweetness but leave sense behind.

With each passing moment, the lines start to blur,
What once felt simple now feels like a stir.
Yet love's sweet dream wraps them in bliss,
As they dance on the edge of a dangerous abyss.

In the laughter they share, a haunting refrain,
The weight of their choices, a shadowed domain.
As time slips away in the haze of their sin,
The forbidden grows stronger, a battle within.

Yet beneath the smiles, the heart starts to ache,
For love that is true, for their own sake.
In the warmth of the night, they sway to the song,
But deep in their hearts, they know this feels wrong.

Dilaech Gaflat

Zakhmi Dil

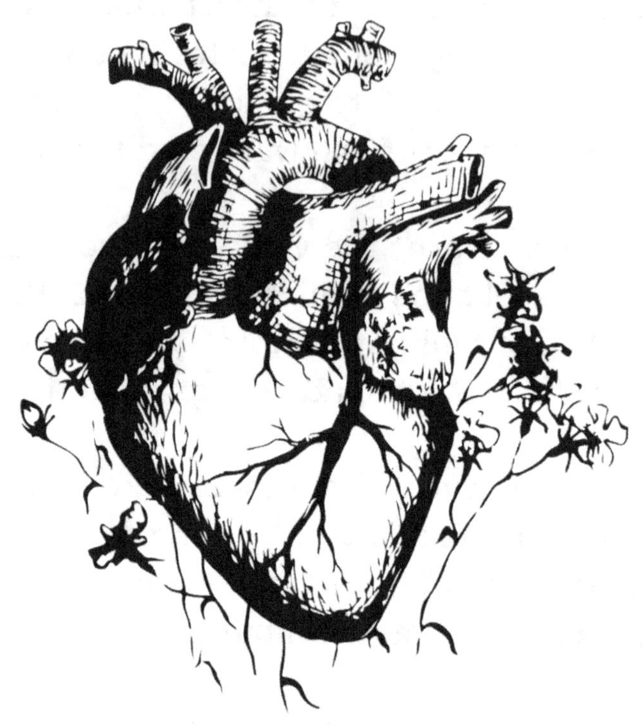

"Indeed, haraam relationships may promise joy, but they only lead to heartbreak and sorrow. True peace lies in the love that's blessed and pure.

As the Dil Kash (attractive) colours of summer began to fade, replaced by the somber hues of Harud (autumn), the love that once brought him joy now cast a shadow over his heart. What had begun as a thrilling adventure filled with laughter and excitement had gradually twisted into a painful reality. The sweetness of their shared moments was now tainted by bitterness, and the thrill of their forbidden love had morphed into a source of constant suffering.

Every time they met, the atmosphere felt charged, not with the electricity of affection, but with an undercurrent of tension that was impossible to ignore. The light hearted banter that once flowed between them had been replaced by sharp words and heated arguments. Their calls, once filled with laughter and dreams of the future, now devolved into accusations and blame.

"Che chuk badleomut" (You've changed) she would say, her voice filled with disappointment.

He would respond, "Naa chei chakh badlemech" (No, you've changed)

The back-and-forth felt like a never-ending cycle, each blaming the other for the failures in their relationship. They were trapped in a toxic cycle, where love turned into a battleground, and the warmth they once shared became overshadowed by bitterness.

It was as if the very essence of their connection had begun to unravel. They had left their friends in search of this intense bond, but now they were alone, without the support that had once lifted them during difficult times.

Zakmi Dil

The familiar faces that had brought them joy and laughter were now distant memories, leaving them to navigate the storm of their relationship on their own.

In their isolation, the boy found himself reflecting on the choices they had made. The Quran's teachings echoed in his mind, a gentle reminder of the boundaries that should not be crossed. He recalled the words that warned against the consequences of indulgence:

"And do not approach unlawful sexual intercourse. Indeed, it is ever an immorality and is evil as a way." (Surah Al-Isra, 17:32)

The reality of their situation weighed heavily on him. The love that once felt so halal and pure now seemed haraam, leading them down a path of destruction. Haraam actions, he realised, would always carry a burden, no matter how deeply one thought they were in love. Their hearts had intertwined, but they were bound by chains of sin, and with each argument, those chains grew tighter, choking the very life out of their connection.

The fights became more frequent, the disagreements more volatile. They would shout at each other, their voices echoing through the quiet places they once cherished. The beautiful landscapes of Kashmir, once a backdrop for their love story, now served as a haunting reminder of their spiralling relationship. The serene beauty around them could not mask the struggle inside.

In one particularly heated exchange, he raised his voice, frustration spilling over. "Che chuy'na aathei yewan buh keecha koshish chus karan" (Why can't you see how hard I'm trying?).

She shot back, tears brimming in her eyes, "koshish? Bronthim heov roud neh wani kihein tih. Che chuk ne suh shakhas, yemes seeth meh mohabat karyav" (Trying? This isn't the same anymore. You're not the person I fell for).

The words stung, each accusation feeling like a knife aimed directly at his heart. Their love, once a source of comfort and joy, had become a war zone of hurt feelings and misunderstandings. The boy could feel the weight of his mistakes, the choices that had led them to this point. The happiness they had shared now felt like a distant memory, replaced by a suffocating darkness.

"And whoever turns away from My remembrance – indeed, he will have a depressed life." (Surah Ta-Ha, 20:124)

The realisation hit him like a cold wave. They were suffocating each other, drowning in their own toxic emotions, and there was no escape in sight. He longed for the days when their laughter echoed like music in the air, but now, their silence felt thundering. The joy of love had been replaced by an unbearable heaviness, and every moment together felt like a reminder of what they had lost.

They had become each other's worst enemies, locked in a cycle of pain. The haraam nature of their relationship became increasingly evident, and he could no longer ignore the worried feeling in his belly.

Zakmi Dil

Love should uplift, but instead, it had become a source of constant trouble. The sweet moments they had shared were overshadowed by a growing sense of dread.

He started to ponder what it meant to love genuinely. The heart, once filled with dreams and hopes, now ached under the weight of reality. The toxicity that had seeped into their relationship made him question whether this love was worth the pain. He found himself longing for clarity, for the kind of love that was built on a foundation of respect, trust, and faith.

As they spent time together, their conversations grew shorter, often punctuated by silence. They both knew something had to change, but neither of them was willing to take the first step. Pride stood in the way, a stubborn barrier that prevented them from reaching out and seeking help. The absence of friends and family only amplified their loneliness, leaving them isolated in their chaos.

In the quiet moments, he would find himself reflecting on the teachings of the Quran, seeking guidance in the midst of chaos. He longed for a way to escape the cycle of pain they had created. The words of Allah offered him solace, a reminder that true love should bring peace, not chaos.

"And He has put love and mercy between your hearts."
(Surah Al-Anfal, 8:63)

The boy realised that without the nikah, their love was like a shaky candle in the wind, weak and easy to blow out. The sweetness of their connection had transformed into bitterness, leaving only regret in its wake.

Zakmi Dil

He began to feel the urgency to address the situation, to find a way to either heal their bond or let it go.

But every time he tried to speak about their struggles, The fear of facing the chaos was very strong. They were trapped in a dance of denial, each waiting for the other to make the first move. The moments of clarity were often drowned out by the noise of their arguments, making it difficult to see a way forward.

As the leaves turned golden and fell from the trees, he sensed that time was running out. The weight of their toxic bond pressed heavily on his chest, and he felt himself longing for the love that once brought him joy. The seasons had changed, and so had their hearts, but he knew that the path to healing lay within reach if they could only find the strength to confront their fears together.

"And Allah is the best of planners." (Surah Al-Imran, 3:54)

He hoped for a resolution, for a chance to rebuild what had been lost. With each passing day, he stuck to the possibility that love could be restored, that perhaps they could break free from the chains of toxicity and rediscover the beauty that had once defined their connection.

But deep down, he also understood that sometimes love means letting go releasing the ties that bind, even when it hurts. As the boy thought about the reality of their relationship, he prepared himself for a difficult journey ahead, one that would require courage and honesty to face the truth of their hearts.

Zakmi Dil

In the warmth of love, where joy used to grow,
Now whispers of sorrow bring a heavy woe.
Once bright were their dreams, now shadows creep,
In the quiet of night, heartache runs deep.

"Loyalty in love," a promise once shared,
Now lost in the chaos, as trust has been scared.
With every harsh word, they drift further apart,
What was once a fire is now a cold heart.

"A sea of tears," they weep in silence,
For the love that has faded, for the pain's violence.
Their laughter feels distant, replaced by the cries,
In the fabric they wove, they unravel their ties.

What happened to the whispers that lit up the night?
What broke the bond that once felt so right?
Each fight grows louder, the distance now wide,
In the dance of their hearts, they've lost the joy inside.

"The book of love," with pages torn out,
Where happiness flourished, now lives only doubt.
What were once gentle touches now cut like a knife,
In the garden of love, only sadness is rife.

As they walk through the ruins of what once was bright,
With every step forward, they meet bitter sights.
But hearts that once fluttered now wear heavy chains,
In the storm of their anger, love quietly wanes.

"Our story," now told through tears and through pain,
Two souls once united now lost in disdain.
Yet still in the darkness, a glimmer may rise,
For even in heartache, hope can disguise.

Zakmi Dil

Tanhaeyi

"In the end, those who love in a haraam way will always leave, for only love rooted in truth and purity can truly stay."

The air around him felt heavy, Burdened with the silence that followed their separation. The Dil Kash Colours of Harud had faded into a dull backdrop, mirroring the emptiness that had settled in his heart. The laughter and warmth that once surrounded him were now distant noises, leaving him in a world that felt completely alone. Every interaction became shallow; no one could see the struggle going on inside him. Deep inside, he would often say, "Kya gov yath zindagi?" (What happened to this life?)

In the weeks that followed their breakup, he looked for peace in solitude. He found himself wandering the streets of Raj Bagh, the familiar sights now tainted with memories of her. Every corner reminded him of shared moments laughter that had once felt so alive now lay buried beneath layers of heartache. The beautiful chaos of life continued around him, but he felt like an outsider looking in, trapped in a bubble of sorrow.

He often spent his evenings driving aimlessly, seeking solace in the quiet of the night. The once serene landscape of Kashmir had turned into a haunting reminder of what he had lost. In those moments of solitude, the world outside seemed to carry on, leaving him stranded in his grief. He would park near Dal Lake, the gentle ripples of the water a stark contrast to the struggles inside him.

"And whoever turns away from My remembrance indeed, he will have a depressed (difficult) life, and We will gather him on the Day of Resurrection blind."
(Surah Ta-Ha, 20:124)

Tanhaeyi

But he found it hard to believe in those words now. Instead, he turned to unhealthy coping mechanisms. From saying, "Bayi, Buh Chus ne cigarette chewan" (brother, I don't smoke cigarettes), cigarettes became a constant companion a means to escape the crushing weight of loneliness. Each drag felt like a brief release, a momentary relief from the pain that enveloped him. The smoke curled into the night air, carrying away his worries but leaving a bitter aftertaste.

Sitting on the edge of the lake, he would watch the water shimmer under the moonlight, feeling a sense of yearning for the connection he had lost. As the stars twinkled above, he would pull out his phone, scrolling through social media feeds filled with laughter and joy, feeling increasingly disconnected from the world.

In the absence of her presence, he sought new connections with strangers, texting random people late into the night. Conversations that began with laughter often devolved into discussions about loneliness and despair. He thought that maybe, just maybe, sharing his feelings with someone anyone could lessen the burden. Yet, he realised that even these interactions were fleeting, failing to fill the void left by her absence.

The darkness of his thoughts grew deeper, spiralling into a cycle of self pity. He would lay awake at night, staring at the ceiling, consumed by memories of her. The moments they shared felt like a cruel joke so vibrant and alive, now transformed into ghosts that haunted his waking hours.

He texted different people, attempting to bridge the gap of loneliness, but each response felt hollow.

Tanhaeyi

It was as if he was searching for validation in a world that had moved on without him. The laughter he once shared with friends felt like a distant memory, overshadowed by the weight of his own sorrow. The emptiness gnawed at him, and with each passing day, he found himself sinking further into despair.

"And do not lose hope in the mercy of Allah."
(Surah Az-Zumar, 39:53)

These words echoed in his mind, but he struggled to grasp their meaning. The pain felt insurmountable, a heavy cloud that obscured any glimmer of hope. He wandered through life like a shadow, disconnected from the vibrant world around him, and no one seemed to notice his absence.

As the nights grew longer, he found himself returning to the familiar spot by the lake, the only place that felt like a shadow of peace. He sat there for hours, thinking the choices that had led him to this point. The quiet of the night was punctuated only by the distant sounds of laughter and joy from gatherings nearby. He felt like an intruder, peering into a world that had once been his.

In these moments, he would often pull out his journal, pouring his heart onto the pages. Poetry became an outlet for the emotions he couldn't express aloud. Each verse reflected the struggle he felt inside, a raw glimpse into his zakhmi dil (broken heart).

In the stillness of night, shadows creep,
Whispers of memories, secrets they keep.
Loneliness wraps around like a shroud,
In the silence, I yearn to cry aloud.

Tanhaeyi

Yet, he remained trapped in this cycle of solitude. The once dil kash conversations with friends had faded into the background. He missed the warmth of companionship, the sense of belonging that had once filled his life.

In an attempt to fill the void, he engaged with strangers online, seeking validation in the form of likes and comments. But the more he reached out, the more isolated he felt. The interactions felt superficial, offering no real connection or comfort. He would often find himself scrolling through pictures of happy faces, feeling a growing sense of resentment toward his own reality.

"Indeed, the soul is at peace with the remembrance of Allah."
(Surah Ar-Ra'd, 13:28)

But in those moments of darkness, he had turned away from that peace. Instead, he found himself in a state of constant searching, trying to grasp something that felt just out of reach. He wandered from one thought to another, never settling, always in pursuit of a fleeting moment of happiness.

The nights were the hardest. The stillness increased his thoughts, and he found himself falling deeper into his loneliness. He often texted friends who were unaware of the depth of his pain, masking his struggles behind a facade of normalcy. But the emptiness continued, troubling his heart and leaving him feeling even more alone.

A heart once full, now shrouded in gloom,
In the silence, I find my own tomb.
Each memory whispers of love turned to pain,
Lost in the shadows, I search for the rain.

Tanhaeyi

He sought comfort in the idea of moving on, yet the very thought filled him with dread. How could he let go of something that had meant so much? The darkness clouded his judgment, making every step forward feel unreachable. The ache of longing twisted in his chest, reminding him that the past could never truly be erased.

As the days turned into weeks, he began to confront the reality of his situation. The loneliness was suffocating, a weight that pressed down on his chest, making it hard to breathe. He needed to find a way out, a path that would lead him back to himself. But with every attempt, he felt the pull of despair tugging at him, threatening to drag him back into the depths. "Kus taawan peow yeath myani zindagi?" (What the heck happened to my life?) he would often say to himself.

In the depths of his loneliness, he began to realise how important it was to reach out for help. The thought scared him, but he knew he couldn't keep living in darkness. He wanted to break free from the cycle of sadness and find a path toward healing.

"And We will surely test you with something of fear and hunger and a loss of wealth and lives and fruits, but give good tidings to the patient."
(Surah Al-Baqarah, 2:155)

These words stayed with him, reminding him that life's challenges were tests. He understood he had to face his pain, allowing himself to grieve the love he had lost. In that moment, he realised it was okay to feel lost, as long as he was willing to seek light again.

Tanhaeyi

Yet, he didn't know that his struggles were only beginning. Unaware of what lay ahead, he tried to reconnect with his innocent past, but confusion clouded his efforts. His life seemed to echo the Kashmiri saying, "Yeoth Wawekh teoth lonekh" (As you sow, so shall you reap).

As he thought about his next steps, he recognised that healing would take time, patience, and a willingness to confront the darkness he had grown used to. Though he felt broken, he knew he had the strength to rebuild, piece by piece.

But he wasn't aware that trying to leave behind what is forbidden wouldn't be easy. The trials would only increase, as Satan would tempt him further, and Allah would test him even more.

In the quiet of shadows, where echoes softly dwell,
A once-bright heart now hides, trapped in its shell.
Wrapped in the stillness, like a blanket of night,
Without laughter around, everything feels tight.

Memories float like whispers in the dark,
Each thought of her smile ignites a tiny spark.
Yet her warmth has faded, leaving a hollow space,
In this deep emptiness, hope begins to race.

"What happened to my heart?" he wonders each day,
As love turns to ashes, slipping away.
With each new sunrise, the weight feels so strong,
In the silence of life, he forgets the song.

He chases the laughter that once filled the air,
Now loneliness surrounds him, too heavy to bear.
He seeks comfort in faith amidst all the pain,
But each moment passes like drops of cold rain.

Thoughts spiral like smoke, swirling in his mind,
As he wanders through memories, feeling confined.
In a crowd of strangers, he still feels alone,
With each new face he meets, he longs for a home.

Drowning in sorrow, with bottles and haze,
Each puff of smoke hides the truth of his days.
"What have I gained?" he questions in despair,
In this chaotic life, where is peace to be found?

Yet deep in the darkness, a spark still remains,
A whisper of hope cutting through sorrowful chains.
For even in loneliness, the heart can still yearn,
To rise from the ashes, to hope and to learn.

Tanhaeyi

Behkaaw

"In hard times, a person may stumble and make mistakes, for these moments are a test from Allah. Through patience and faith, the soul finds strength to rise again."

Behkaaw

By the calm banks of Dal Lake, he felt himself slipping away from the person he used to be. Once bright and full of life, he now felt numb and empty. The pull of a new crowd by the lake had drawn him into a world he hadn't imagined a world where he tried to escape his pain with things that made him feel dull and lost. Each time, it felt like he was losing more of himself.

Every evening, he would wander back to the lake, where the moonlight shimmered on the water, offering a sense of calm he longed for. But while the lake seemed peaceful, his heart was full of chaos. Surrounded by new people, he started turning to drugs and alcohol, hoping they could take away the darkness he felt inside. The laughter and friendship around him felt comforting, but the relief didn't last. Each time, he was left feeling emptier, craving more to fill the growing emptiness within him.

With these new people around him, he forgot the values he once held dear. The elders who had guided him through life were now just distant memories, their advice ignored as he sank further into this wild way of living. He often spoke harshly, his words sharp and unkind a big change from the gentle boy he used to be.

The warmth of family felt like a far-off memory, replaced by the cold hold of addiction. He pulled away from those who cared for him, shutting out loved ones who worried about how much he'd changed. Friends who once shared happy times with him now looked on with concern as he slipped further into this new life, one shaped by bad influences and the escape offered by harmful substances.

Behkaaw

The nights became a blur of endless escapes. The excitement of drugs quickly turned into a craving he couldn't control. Each high brought a short moment of happiness, but the fall afterward was painful, leaving him with a deep emptiness he couldn't shake. What he once turned to for comfort now held him prisoner, trapping him in a cycle of sadness and regret.

He wandered the streets at night, lost in his thoughts, searching for places that matched the chaos inside him. In the city's shadows, he felt a strange thrill, but it was an empty kind of life a mask hiding the pain he carried. The laughter of new friends sounded empty, lacking any real warmth, and only made him feel lonelier.

Days turned into weeks, and weeks turned into months, and with every moment, he fell deeper into darkness. The drugs took over his life, telling him false stories that made him forget the reality he once loved. The lively boy he used to be, full of dreams and hope, faded away into a dull life where his only friends were substances that gave him a short escape from the chaos in his mind.

One fateful night, as he stumbled home, the remnants of intoxication clouding his judgment, he encountered an auto driver waiting for a fare. The driver, sensing the chaos in the boy's eyes, attempted to engage him. "Near Khodai karnei hidayth," he said, hoping to reach out. "May Allah guide you to the right path."

But those words didn't touch him. The boy, trapped in a cloud of anger and confusion, shouted back, hurling insults without thinking. The driver, surprised, simply shook his head, sadness on his face as he said, "Kya gov saanei Kasheeri?" (What happened to our valley, Kashmir?) before driving away.

Behkaaw

The boy's heart felt heavy with sadness, but he didn't see how far he had strayed from who he really was.

With each passing day, the drugs took a bigger role in his life. What had started as a thrill turned into a strong addiction, pushing him further away from the boy he used to be. He stopped feeling the love of his family and the warmth that had once surrounded him. Instead, he became a source of worry for his family, who watched helplessly as their son fell into darkness. The name that had once brought pride in the community started to lose its respect with every careless choice he made.

His parents would sit late into the night, their soft voices filled with worry as they talked about their son's change. They remembered the laughter, the hope, and the dreams they had for him. "Kyah gov Sanis khane maelis?" (What happened to our boy?) "Khoda zaaneih kemisenz nazar lajes" (Allah knows whose evil eye is upon him), his mother would say quietly, sadness in her voice. Each tear she shed felt like a sharp pain in his heart, but he was too far gone to reach out, too lost to care.

The streets he once walked with friends had become a maze of shame and darkness. He would pass familiar faces that used to greet him with smiles, but now they looked away or felt sorry for him. "Aakeh hasav aaw shodeh" (here comes the addict), those who once admired him would say. The whispers of worry followed him, reminding him of how far he had fallen.

The cycle continued: nights spent in a haze of drugs, mornings filled with regret, and evenings that merged into nights again. He lost touch with friends, with the world around him.

Behkaaw

The vibrant life of youth, once filled with potential, faded into a bleak existence where his only companions were substances that offered a temporary reprieve from the chaos in his mind.

The life he was leading was not only a disservice to himself but also a painful reality for his family. The fear of losing everything they had worked for consumed him, yet he felt trapped in a cycle of addiction that was suffocating him.

The weight of his choices felt like a heavy stone pressing down on him. He looked at the water, which showed the chaos inside him. It was then that he saw his own reflection, and for the first time in a long while, he felt a quick flash of recognition a moment where he saw the boy he used to be.

In that moment, he felt the first signs of regret, a faint glimmer of hope buried deep beneath his addiction. He realized he couldn't keep going down this path; he had to find a way back to who he used to be. But the idea of change seemed overwhelming, and the road ahead was filled with challenges.

He had turned away from the light, but perhaps it wasn't too late to find his way back. Perhaps, just perhaps, he could seek forgiveness and reclaim the life he had lost.

Behkaaw

In the twilight of dreams where shadows play,
He dances with darkness, losing his way.
"New winds are blowing," he thinks with a sigh,
With strangers like stars lighting up the sky.

Whispers of pleasure call out like a game,
In the heart of the city, he feels all the same.
"How do I forget?" he wonders tonight,
As he dives deeper, surrendering to night.

Amidst all the laughter, the highs and the lows,
He trades in his spirit for a false sense of glow.
New friends bring their troubles, tempting him to sin,
With every moment of joy, he gets pulled further in.

"The path I walk on" feels lost and unclear,
As he stumbles through choices, swallowed by fear.
What once felt like freedom is now a dark chain,
With each puff of smoke, he dances with pain.

In the depths of the night, where shadows unite,
He's lost all direction, caught up in the fight.
"A tired heart," he thinks, heavy and worn,
In search of a high, he's ignored the dawn.

Yet beneath all the temptations, his heart still cries,
In this chaos around him, he questions the lies.
"What's happening inside?" he wonders with dread,
In the wave of new winds, he feels hope ahead.

For even when darkness fills up his mind,
A spark of redemption is waiting to find.
In every new struggle, a lesson might dwell,
To seek out the truth and break free from the spell.

Behkaaw

AZEEZ

"When a person walks a difficult or misguided path, it is the mother's heart that bears the deepest sorrow, for no one feels their child's pain more than she does."

Azeez

In the quiet corners of their home, a heavy silence hung in the air, broken only by the soft cries of a mother whose heart ached for her son. Each evening, as darkness fell, she would sit alone in the dim light, her hands raised in prayer, asking Allah to help bring her boy back to the right path. The weight of her worry was like a heavy blanket, wrapping around her as she recalled the joyful moments they once shared. She longed for the days when laughter filled their home and her son smiled with hope, not the sadness that now filled her heart.

Khodai diyne towfeek," (may Allah guide him) she whispered through her tears, her voice shaking with both hope and sadness. She remembered the boy she once knew the bright-eyed child full of dreams and innocence. Her heart hurt as she saw him slipping away into addiction, lost in substances that took away his spirit. Every time he came home in a daze, seeing him brought a flood of sorrow, and she would quietly go to her room, looking for comfort in her prayers.

On many nights, she would sit on the edge of her bed, holding her prayer beads and reciting verses from the Quran about mercy and guidance. Her tears fell like rain, each drop a quiet request for her son's return to a better life. She felt helpless as she saw the change in the boy who once filled their home with laughter. The darkness of addiction covered his once bright spirit, and she realised that she could not save him by herself. All she could do was pray.

Then came a day like no other a day when the darkness felt a little lighter, even if just for a moment. He woke up early in the morning, with the sun shining through the window and filling the room with a warm light.

Azeez

He rubbed his eyes and took a deep breath, surprised to realise he wasn't in a fog, not high on drugs, but sober and clear headed for the first time in what felt like forever.

As he walked through the house, he heard soft crying coming from his mother's room. He knocked gently on the door and stepped inside, and what he saw hit him hard. There she sat, her head in her hands, tears flowing down her cheeks. The sight shook him, breaking through the numbness he had wrapped himself in.

"Mooji cze kyaze wadaan?" (Why are you crying, Mom?) he asked softly, his voice barely above a whisper.

She looked up, her eyes red and puffy from crying, but he could see a flicker of hope in them. "Gabra kas wane teh kus bozyam?" (Son, who should I tell and who will listen?) she replied, her voice cracking as she pointed to her heart. "Mea che dilas zaed gameit." (There are holes in my heart.) "Lagya balai che kemsenz nazar lajei." (May I die for you, whose evil eye is on you?) "Che has chuk roomut." (You are lost.) "Bas wanei Cheh seth tem sei mangan waps." (Now I'm asking Allah to bring you back.)

In that moment, something shifted inside him. The weight of her words hit him, and he felt the first signs of understanding wash over him. He had been so caught up in his own problems that he hadn't noticed how much they affected the people who cared about him.

"Gas temsenz waatih kun waps," she said, her hands shaking as she took her tasbiyah. "Turn back to Allah, my son". "He is always waiting for you with open arms."

Azeez

The sincerity in her eyes and the depth of her pain touched him deeply. For the first time, he really listened, letting her words reach the broken parts of his heart. "Mooji," he said, his voice shaking, "Buh haa badle mooji" (I will change, Mom). "Buh naa roozeh waneh yeoth kenh" (I won't be like this anymore).

She took his hands in hers, her grip firm yet gentle. "Meyon khoda diyih himat myani gobra" (My God will give you strength, my son). "He will guide you if you seek Him with an open heart. Roab chuna paanei wanan" (Allah is saying this Himself). "Inna ma'al usri yusra" (With hardship comes ease).

As he sat beside her, listening to her prayers, a feeling of clarity started to grow inside him. He realised that his mother's tears were not just tears of sadness they were also tears of strong love. Love that had lasted through the hardest times, hope that had battled against despair.

In that vulnerable moment, he understood that he could no longer go on this path of destruction. Her tears showed him the pain of his choices, and he felt the walls he had built around his heart starting to fall apart.

"Wuni chui mookeh path fear timov cheezov nish yem che noksaan chei watnawan," she urged, her voice steady. "You still have a chance; stay away from the things that harm you. You have the power to choose, my son. The choice is yours."

He nodded, feeling the weight of her words sink deep into his heart. In that delicate moment between mother and son, a seed of hope began to grow. The road ahead would be full of challenges, but he knew he wouldn't have to walk it alone.

Azeez

As he looked into her eyes, he saw the love that had always been there, waiting patiently for him to return. The pain in her heart became his own, a shared burden that connected them in ways he had long forgotten.

"Lagai Balai Mooji," he whispered, expressing the deep bond between them. "Aaze keh baad traav buh har kanh galat kaaem," (From today, I will leave every bad habit) he promised, his voice filled with determination.

In that moment, he understood that turning back to Allah wasn't something he had to do alone; it was a journey they could share together. For the first time in a long while, he felt a small spark of hope inside him a hope that maybe, just maybe, he could find his way back to who he once was, guided by the strong love of a mother who would never give up on him.

In the quiet of night, where shadows run deep,
A mother's heart aches, as she weeps and she weeps.
"God's mercy," she whispers, her prayers take flight,
For her son lost in darkness, trapped in the night.

With trembling hands, she lifts her voice high,
In the silence of sorrow, she lets out a sigh.
"O Lord, our guide," she calls with a plea,
In this time of trial, she counts what it costs to be free.

Her tears flow like rivers, cutting through the dark,
Each drop a prayer, a small glowing spark.
"From Your grace, dear God," she humbly implores,
She seeks strength for her son, who's lost in his wars.

As he wanders through shadows, unaware of her pain,
She dreams of the day when he'll break every chain.
"The state of my heart," her silent wish beams,
In her prayers, she finds comfort, and hope gently gleams.

One morning he stirs, waking from a deep sleep,
To find her beside him, her vigil to keep.
"Why are you crying, Mom?" he softly inquires,
She shares her heart's whispers, igniting his fires.

"Return to your roots," she urges with love,
In the depths of despair, there's hope from above.
With her prayer beads in hand, she talks to the sky,
"Lead him on the right path," she calls, raising her cry.

For a mother's love knows no limits or end,
In the storms of his life, she'll always defend.
Through the prayers of her heart, the shadows will fade,
"God's mercy," she believes, a promise remade.

Azeez

Aahh Guzaeri

"Emerging from the darkest phase, the journey toward light is often the hardest, for true growth demands strength through every step."

As the first light of morning filled the sky, the world around him began to wake up. For the boy, it felt like a fresh start. He had been lost in darkness for so long, trapped in feelings of sadness and addiction. But now, standing at the edge of a new beginning, he could sense a small light breaking through the heavy clouds that had covered his life. It was a feeling he hadn't experienced in a long time hope.

The struggles were tough. Every day felt like a fight against the shadows of his past against the pull of drugs that once seemed like a way out. He would wake up in the morning, his heart feeling heavy from the weight of his choices. The cravings nagged at him, promising a moment of relief, but he fought back, determined not to give in.

His mother's words, "Inna ma'al usri yusra" (Surely with hardship comes ease), echoed in his mind, reminding him that there was hope. He would sit up in bed, tears rolling down his cheeks as he poured out his heart to Allah. "Ya Allah, help me," he cried, feeling exposed and vulnerable. No longer did he want comfort from temporary pleasures his heart now longed for something much deeper and more meaningful.

With each tear that fell, he felt a weight lift. Each cry was a release, a cleansing of the soul. He was beginning to understand that true strength came not from avoiding pain, but from embracing it and seeking solace in Allah's mercy. As he fought against the darkness, he was finding himself again a version of himself that had been buried beneath layers of shame and despair.

Aahh Guzaeri

His newfound love was not for another person or the temporary high that came with it. Instead, he was falling deeply in love with Allah, with the divine presence that had always been there, waiting patiently for him to return. "Wa a'lamu anna Allaha Ghafoorun Raheem" (And know that Allah is Forgiving and Merciful) became his wazeef (mantra), wrapping around his heart like a warm hug.

The boy found comfort in the verses of the Quran, each one a light guiding his way. "Ya ayyuha allatheena amanoo istajeeboo lillahi walirrasooli idha da'akum lima yuhyeekum" (O you who have believed, respond to Allah and to the Messenger when he calls you to that which gives you life) stirred something deep inside him. This was the call he had been waiting for an invitation to truly live.

Every moment he spent in prayer was an act of defiance against the darkness that had once consumed him. He would rise before the sun, sitting in quiet reflection, his heart whispering words of gratitude. "Rabbi zidni 'ilm" (My Lord, increase me in knowledge) became a plea not just for understanding, but for strength to persevere. He longed to deepen his connection with Allah, to learn about His mercy, love, and guidance.

As he moved away from the negativity of his past, he found new friends who were also on their path to healing. Together, they would meet, sharing their stories of struggle and victory, each story adding to a beautiful picture of hope. They would recite verses from the Quran, with each word making them stronger. "Wa man ja'a bilhasanati falaahu khayrun minha" (And whoever comes with a good deed will have better than it) became a guiding light, encouraging him to focus on the good that could come from his past mistakes.

Aahh Guzaeri

With each day that went by, he felt the hold of addiction getting weaker, the chains that had once held him breaking away. The battle was not easy, but with every small victory, he felt a rush of hope. "Udhkhulu fee silmikaafah" (Enter into Islam completely) became his guiding phrase, reminding him that he was on a journey to become whole, accepting his faith fully and without hesitation.

One evening, as he walked by the banks of Dal Lake, he paused to admire the sunset. The sky was filled with shades of orange and pink, creating a beautiful scene. It reminded him of the beauty in the world that he had once ignored. In that moment, he felt a strong sense of gratitude, realising that even with his struggles, there were still many blessings around him.

"Ya Allah, I am thankful for this new start," he whispered as the light began to fade, feeling the warmth of His presence around him. "You take one step towards Me, and I will take two towards you." This promise echoed in his heart, reminding him that he was never truly alone.

In his heart, he started to understand how deep Allah's love truly was a love that went beyond sin and forgiveness. "Indeed, Allah loves those who repent and loves those who are pure" (Surah Al-Baqarah, 2:222) echoed in his mind, filling him with the strength to keep moving forward.

With each day that went by, he learned to accept the struggle, realising that healing wasn't a straight path but had its ups and downs. He leaned on his faith, finding strength in prayer and the support of others.

Aahh Guzaeri

He was rediscovering himself, not just as a boy lost in darkness but as a cherished servant of Allah, someone seeking truth and light.

As he stood at the edge of the lake, watching the reflection of the sun dip below the horizon, he felt a sense of hope ignite within him. The journey was far from over, but now he was walking with purpose guided by the love of Allah, ready to face whatever challenges lay ahead.

"Rabbana atina fidunya hasanatan wa fil akhirati hasanatan wa qina 'adhabannar" (Our Lord, grant us good in this world and good in the Hereafter, and save us from the torment of the Fire) became his prayer, a reminder of the balance he sought in life.

In that moment, he realised he wasn't just looking for a little light; he was welcoming it, letting it fill his heart and light up his way. The boy who had once been lost in darkness was now stepping into the light, ready to embrace life again, guided by faith and love.

Aahh Guzaeri

In the depths of despair, where shadows once lay,
A flicker of hope starts to light up the way.
"After darkness, there's light," a truth we hold dear,
In the heart of the lost, a new spark appears.

He rises from the ashes, tears glistening bright,
In the stillness of prayer, he learns to find light.
"O Allah, Your mercy," a lifeline so near,
With each heartfelt prayer, he casts away fear.

As he looks to the heavens, seeking comfort anew,
His heart beats in rhythm with the One who is true.
"O my Lord, guide me," he asks through his strife,
In the fight against darkness, he rediscovers life.

The love once misplaced now blossoms like a flower,
In the arms of the Divine, he finds strength and power.
"God's promise," he remembers, a bond that will mend,
Through pain and through trials, he finds a true friend.

Each morning he wakes, with an open heart wide,
No longer a wanderer, he walks with pride.
"A ray of light," in every dawn's glow,
Guides him towards hope, where new dreams will grow.

The whispers of guidance, soft echoes of grace,
In moments of struggle, he sees Heaven's face.
"Show me the way," he pleads with a heart,
In the light of Your love, he chooses to start.

Now love for the Creator fills every part,
Restoring the innocence that once left his heart.
"Thank You, O God," he sings with joy,
In the journey of healing, he finds his true joy.

Aahh Guzaeri

Nooruk Safar

"When you discover the path of light, life unfolds with ease, blooming like a flower; every moment of despair fades away, feeling insignificant in the beauty of newfound joy."

As the sun rose over the peaceful beauty of Kashmir, the boy sat quietly in his room, feeling calm and safe like being wrapped in a warm blanket. The dark memories of his past were slowly fading away, and he began to understand that his struggles had brought him to a better place. He could feel hope filling his heart, lighting up the areas that had once been filled with sadness.

"Alhamdulillah," he whispered, feeling thankful like a gentle stream flowing from his heart. He thought about the hard times that had tested him, but he now saw that each challenge was a step toward understanding himself and his faith better. With every breath, he felt a stronger bond with Allah, who was the source of all his strength and guidance.

Determined to change, he stepped outside and into the morning sun, which bathed the valley in a golden light. The air felt fresh and cool, filled with the sweet smell of blooming flowers and the promise of new beginnings. He walked toward the local mosque, a place that had once felt strange but now felt warm and welcoming. The sounds of the call to prayer echoed in his heart, awakening something special within him.

As he entered the mosque, he was greeted by the warmth of the community. Faces lit up with smiles, reflecting the shared joy of faith and fellowship. He felt an overwhelming sense of belonging, realising that he was not alone in his struggles. The laughter of children echoed around him, reminding him of the innocence he had longed to reclaim.

Kneeling on the prayer mat, he closed his eyes and poured out his heart to Allah. "Ya Allah, forgive me for my past, and guide me on this new path. Help me to be a source of light for others, just as You have been for me." The words flowed from his lips, each one carrying the weight of his past and the hope for a brighter future.

In that moment of sincere supplication, he recalled the verse from the Quran, "Wa man ja'a bilhasanati falaahu khayrun minha" (And whoever comes with a good deed will have better than it). He understood that every act of kindness he performed, every moment of patience he exhibited, would lead him to something far greater than he could imagine. The knowledge filled him with a sense of purpose; he wanted to do good, to uplift those around him.

With renewed energy, he decided to write. He gathered his thoughts and began to pour his experiences onto the pages of a journal. The ink flowed effortlessly as he recounted his journey from darkness to light, capturing the essence of his struggles, his mistakes, and the lessons learned along the way. Each word was a cathartic release, a way to articulate the changes he felt within.

"Rabbana atina fidunya hasanatan wa fil akhirati hasanatan wa qina 'adhabannar" (Our Lord, grant us good in this world and good in the Hereafter, and save us from the torment of the Fire) became his guiding prayer as he wrote. He poured his heart into each entry, reflecting on how far he had come. The boy who once sought validation through fleeting pleasures now yearned for a connection that was profound and everlasting..

Nooruk Safar

Days turned into weeks, and he became more involved in his community. He volunteered at the local center, helping to organize events and support those in need. The smiles of the children he met brought him a joy he hadn't felt in a long time. He began to see how important it was to help others, realising that by caring for those around him, he was also healing his own pain.

His relationship with his family grew stronger. He worked hard to connect with them, sharing his thoughts and feelings and listening to their advice. He treasured the time spent with his mother, whose love had always been a guiding light in his life. "Mooji, I'm sorry for the pain I caused you," he would say, tears in his eyes. She would hug him tightly, her heart filled with love and forgiveness.

"Gobra meah wanyawoui che rob chu wanen paaneh" (My son, I told you that Allah is saying Himself) "Inna ma'al usri yusra" (Indeed, with hardship comes ease). "Yeuth che hidayat kornei khoda karetan saarnei" (The way He blessed you, may He bless others too). He understood that Allah's mercy was everywhere and that the struggles he had faced were important for his growth. The darkness had turned into a new strength, and he felt lighter, free from the chains that had once held him back.

The evenings turned into a time for thinking and praying. He would sit by Dal Lake, watching the sun set behind the mountains. In those quiet moments, he would recite verses from the Quran, letting the words wash over him like a soft breeze. The calm water reflected the peace he felt inside.

"Ya Allah, I am grateful for this peace. Help me stay strong in my faith," he would whisper. He knew that this peace was a gift that needed care and commitment.

Nooruk Safar

As he grew spiritually, he discovered happiness in sharing his story with others. He started to mentor younger people who were facing similar struggles. He listened to their stories, offered advice, and encouraged them to find comfort in faith. "You are not alone," he would tell them, remembering his own journey. "There is always hope, even in the darkest times."

He became a source of hope for others who had lost their way. He understood that his past struggles could inspire others, showing them the strength that comes from facing challenges and the kindness of Allah.

With each passing day, he felt more at peace with himself and his choices. The boy who once sought fulfillment in fleeting pleasures had transformed into a young man grounded in faith, love, and compassion. He learned to appreciate the beauty of life, finding joy in the simple moments the laughter of friends, the warmth of family, and the tranquility of prayer.

"Alhamdulillah for this life," he would often say, feeling thankful from the bottom of his heart. The love he had for Allah was now mixed with the love he felt for the people around him. He understood that real happiness didn't come from seeking quick pleasures but from the relationships he built and the kindness he shared with others.

As the sun sank below the horizon, filling the sky with deep shades of blue, he felt a sense of fulfilment like never before. He had discovered his peace and purpose, and he was ready to welcome the journey ahead with an open heart.

"Indeed, every struggle was worth it, for it led me to this moment of clarity and peace," he mused, a smile gracing his lips. He was ready to face whatever came next, armed with the knowledge that he was never truly alone on this Nooruk Safar, the path of light.

Nooruk Safar

In the silence of prayer, where whispers take flight,
A heart once in turmoil now basks in the light.
"Peace of the heart," he feels in a warm embrace,
In the arms of the Divine, he finally finds his place.

From shadows of sorrow to mountains so high,
With faith as his anchor, he learns how to fly.
"God's kindness," he knows, is a love that won't cease,
In the depths of his struggle, he finds sweet release.

Each verse of the Qur'an soothes his weary soul,
Restoring his spirit, making him whole.
"You are always with me," he feels in each grace,
With every breath taken, he knows he's embraced.

He reflects on the trials that shaped who he's become,
In the woven tapestry, he sees what's to come.
"Everything is by God's will," he smiles with a twist,
Through pain and the lessons, nothing goes amiss.

With gratitude flowing, he counts every blessing,
In laughter's soft echoes and love's gentle dressing.
"Thank You, O God, in every situation," he sings,
He finds peace in his heart, where stillness brings wings.

No longer a stranger to both joy and pain,
He walks through the valleys, dances in the rain.
"God's light," he discovers, is a guide that won't fade,
In the love of his Creator, his worries are laid.

Now tales of his journey spread wide and far,
Inspiring the lost, like a shining star.
"My story of faith," he shares with a smile,
In the battle for peace, he's found his true style.

With every new dawn comes a chance to begin,
In the warmth of his heart, where the light pours in.
"Thank you, my Lord, for guiding me home,"
In the sanctuary of love, forever he'll roam.

Nooruk Safar

Thank You

As I conclude this journey through Nooruk Safar, I want to extend my heartfelt gratitude to each reader who has taken the time to explore this story. Your support means the world to me. Writing this book has been a transformative experience, not just in sharing my thoughts but also in understanding the depths of human emotion and the importance of faith.

I hope that this narrative resonates with you and inspires reflection on your own journeys. May you find strength in your struggles and joy in your discoveries.

Thank you for being a part of this journey.

"Special thanks to Muzamil Gull for assisting me with the Kashmiri words and titles."

In every darkness, there is a path to light;
embrace it, and let your spirit soar.

— Mutahir Showkat

The End